THAT VOICE INSIDE MY HEAD

Ines Rue

Copyright © 2022 by Ines Rue

All rights reserved.

No portion of this book may be reproduced in any form without written permission from the publisher or author, except as permitted by U.S. copyright law.

Contents

	Chapter	1
1.	#1 A Shadow at my window	2
2.	#2 Run	9
3.	#3 Bound	13
4.	#4 Fighting Felix	17
5.	#5 One of the Same	19
6.	#6 Lost	21
7.	#7 Truth, Dare, or Die	22
8.	#8 The Smallest Spark	26
9.	#9 Thief	28
10.	#10- Psycho	31
11.	#11 Test	34
12.	#12 Nightmares are Real	38
13.	#13 My Permission	40
14.	#14 Math Class	42
15.	#15 Enemies on Earth	45

16.	#16 Deals	49
17.	#17 Home Coming	60
18.	#18 Served Cold	65
19.	#19 Vengance	67
20.	#20- Fury and Resolution	72
21.	#21 Horrible Perfection	75

It all started with a game of truth, dare, or die and escalated from there. But every relationship has its ups and downs and Abigail and Peter are no exception. After Abigail realizes that she is a target of something big, she knows that she put herself and Pan in danger. So she leaves and returns to the land without magic. But what happens when Pan looks for her- and finds her. After all, no one is allowed to leave Neverland without his permission.

#1 A Shadow at my window

"Who can tell me what the French and Indian war was fought over? Miss Black?" My teacher, Mrs. Din, nodded towards me, the best student in the class.

"The Ohio River Valley and fur trade, ma'am," I answered without missing a beat.

"Very good, Abigail," she congratulated and scribbled my answer on the whiteboard, "And who can tell me about the impact this had on the colonies? How about you?"

Some kid I didn't know answered, but he was wrong. Mrs. Din went to find someone else to answer when a lady working in the school's main office stepped into the classroom.

"Mrs. Din? Abigail Black's mother is here to pick her up from school."

"Well go on!" Mrs. Din said to me with a motion towards the door, "You heard her. Read pages 34-47 in your textbook tonight!"

I gathered my things clumsily and hurried out of the room after the lady from the office. I heard the faint voice of Mrs. Din calling on Jimmy Miller as I left. "What's she picking me up for?"

THAT VOICE INSIDE MY HEAD

"She didn't say much. Some sort of family emergency." Answered the uptight lady. She was clad in black heels, a black pencil skirt, a white blouse, red lipstick, and some sort of bun for her hair. She carried a notebook in one hand and a ballpoint pen in the other. She had a tense expression with lines across her face that showed how stressed she normally was, but also revealed that she knew more than she was letting on.

"You know what the emergency was. What happened?" I pressed. An anxious, unsettling feeling washed over me. What was so important that she wouldn't tell me?

The woman's fast, confident stride broke as she paused, but she shook her head and kept moving as she did before. "How did you know I knew?"

"I'm good at reading people. What happened?"

We continued down the tiled floors of the school's halls, the lady's heels click, click, clicking with each step. Each click sounded like the tick of a time bomb. Click, click, click, tick, tick, tick. What would I find when the bomb finally went off?

"I can't say, Abigail. But you can discuss it with your mother when you see her."

"Step-mom,"

"Regardless, you can discuss it with her when you see her. Which is now."

She was right. We turned the corner to reach the main office. Inside, my stepmom was sitting on a chair, tapping her manicured nails on her phone's glittery case. God, how I hated her. Bile rose to my throat every time I saw her.

Ever since my real mother abandoned my dad and me, it had just been me and him having fun. Most of the time time. I did commit a crime or two once and awhile, but my troubled life was hidden easily at school with a polished smile and the correct answers on the test. No one suspects the most brilliant, perfect girl in school that's good at everything to be living in hell at home.

But my dad helped me stay strong. Then one day, he came home with that good for nothing leech because she could provide financial support for our family and expected me to accept her as a mother. Well, I didn't, even when they married. My stepmom always hated me. That may have been justifiable since I hated her, you have to expect her to be a jerk back. Nevertheless, she never ceased to verbally abuse me at every turn. But I put up with her because my dad and I needed her.

"Hi, honey," chimed my stepmom with a smile that was creepily wide enough to go from happy to psychotic. She was clearly angry at me but was putting on an act in front of the other adults. "Come on, we're leaving!"

I glanced back down the halls of Franklyn High, wishing I could run back to my history class in the safety of schooling, but I was smart enough to know that there was no way to resist. I had tried before when I was younger. It didn't end well.

THAT VOICE INSIDE MY HEAD

My stepmom seized my wrist and escorted me out of the building and into the car. "What's going on?" I asked, tossing my backpack into the backseat.

"Your dad is dead," she flipped on her blinked and turned on to the next street, not batting an eye.

It took a moment for me to process what she was saying, but when I finally managed to speak, I gasped out a feeble, "What?"

"He died. Some sort of drunk driver hit him. We took him to the hospital, but he died. When we get home, you have to take out the trash. Don't forget." Her tone clearly showed she didn't care about her husband's death. A wretched woman, she was. Simply wretched.

I felt my defensives crumbling as I thought about my dad and my stepmom. "How can you do that? How can you say that? How can you not care that my father, your husband died? How repulsive are you?" Tears brimmed in my eyes, but I refused to let them fall. I would not let this monster see me cry.

"Watch your mouth, you filthy brat!" she scolded, as if everything was normal, as if my world hadn't just fallen apart, as if my dad wasn't dead. "You watch it, or I'll wash it out with soap! Now, take out the trash and do the dishes. I am going out with friends tonight."

I was so emotionally numb that I didn't even say something sassy, like, "You have friends?" and instead leaned my head against the glass pane on the car window.

How could my dad be gone? Just like that? This morning, we were talking at the breakfast table about signing my permission slip for my science field trip next week. He had laughed and joked with me since my stepmom was upstairs doing her hair and couldn't dampen the mood. My dad gave me a kiss on the forehead and waved me goodbye as I went to the school bus after telling me to have a good day.

How was I supposed to have a good day when now he's just... dead. Not "passed away" or "moved on" or "gone", or any other watered-down expression. He was dead. Nothing more, nothing less.

And now I was left with my stepmom, a person I hated with every fiber in my being. Of course, if I had told my dad this, he would have smiled softly and said, "Abby, don't say that. Yes, Marshal can be difficult, but she is my wife now. I know you don't like her, I'm not asking you to like her. Just tolerate her, okay?" Even though I despised those words, I would pay anything to hear him whisper them again, to hear his voice.

Our car turned into our driveway. Biting back tears, I grabbed my backpack to run inside. Immediately, I dashed up the stairs to break down in my room.

Sobbing hysterically, I fell to the floor, clutching my clothes and shaking. Gasps of breath came out between all my weeping, but I didn't care. All I could think of is that the only person that loved me is dead. Without my dad, I was lost. Completely and utterly lost.

I wish the bomb never went off.

~+~

As time progressed, Marshal didn't change. She was still an "evil stepmother" type of person, and completely unbearable. She made a point to call me sexist slurs, insult my appearance (including weight acne, hair color, skin color, and eye color), discredit anything I did

THAT VOICE INSIDE MY HEAD 7

and generally put me down about anything and everything. No one understood, not even my friend Lucile.

"I just don't know what to do, Lucile," I sighed to her after expressing how my stepmom treated me as we walked to English together. "She's terrible to me."

"Well, at least she doesn't physically hurt you. It could be worse, Abigail." Lucile said distractedly. "My aunt grew up in an abusive home. Her parents hit her and threw her out on the streets. That's real abuse. Your mom is just rude. Be thankful you're not my aunt."

I did not know how to reply to her. Because how do you tell a friend that thinks she is helping that she is only making you more lost? Lost in despair, lost in misunderstanding, lost in a sea of hatred hellbent on drowning you. How do you say that you would rather die than continue to be lost? That's just it, you couldn't.

So, as usual, I hid behind a smile and a sarcastic remark, "Yeah, thank god I'm not your aunt. Then I'd be related to you!"

Lucile laughed and smacked my arm. "Oh, shut up!"

The two of us continued on to English, joking the whole way.

~+~

6 Months Later

If there was one thing I thought would never happen to me, it's having a shadow-type-thing standing at my window. Talking to me.

I guess there's a first time for everything?

"Come with me. Take my hand." The shadow was extending its hand, or is it really a hand considering that's it's a shadow. Who's to say that shadows call them hands? The world may never know.

I looked at the shadow's hand (if it really is a hand) and looked back up into its glowing blue eyes. I took a deep breath and said, "Okay. You come to my window and creepily open it and try to abduct me. And you are a shadow. And you're talking. Do you honestly think that I am going ANYWHERE with you?"

Apparently shadows don't like being smack talked to, because it grabbed my wrist and yanked me out the window and started flying while I was screaming like an idiot. Well, today sucked.

#2 Run

You may be saying, "Oh my gosh, Abigail! I can't believe that you have been abducted by a shadow! Are you okay?" And if you happened to ask such a pathetic question, then considering I was just dropped on a beach from, like, 100 feet in the air, yes, I'm simply amazing.

I stood and looked up to where the shadow had been. It had flown far off and I wasn't about to chase it, I was never one to enjoy running anyway.

Also, in case you are wondering, no, I am not delusional. I really was on some beach and I really was dropped by a shadow, I swear.

"God, that sounds really crazy," I muttered to myself, "Abducted by a shadow? Sounds like a little kid's story."

But after pinching myself, I was very sure that this was, unfortunately, real.

"I have had enough freakishness for one day, thank you very much," I mumbled again. So I did what any sane person would do. I started into the dark ominous woods that were in front of my face that seemed to scream DANGER! Great decision, I know.

I wandered for a good hour, seeing nothing but trees and plants, before it started to get dark. Actually, come to think of it, it was always pretty dark, but now it was darker than it was before.

Glaring at the sky, I began to collect large branches for a lean-to, mumbling frustrated curses at the sky, even though I knew that was stupid. The brush in the surrounding area was thick and there were some good sized branches that must have fallen after a storm. They would make a good frame, and the foliage would be a good cover.

After eons, I finally completed the structure (that if I was honest with myself, was a really crappy structure) so that I could pile large leaves over the top to block any rain that might fall. Worn out, I crawled underneath and dusted my hands on my ripped jeans to lean against the tree.

The air was cold and the shelter was drafty, making me hug my legs closer to myself. Somewhere in the distance, I though I heard whooping and hollering.

"Probably an animal," I whispered to myself, picking at a lose thread on my jeans.

Another gust of wind blew through the cracks of my lean-to. I began softy muttering some choice words to myself as I pondered the events of the day. A shadow doesn't just, kinda', decide to go kidnap someone and drop them on an island in the middle of freaking nowhere anymore than random teens appear from the woods with big clubs. But of course both of those happened. Lucky me.

THAT VOICE INSIDE MY HEAD 11

While the boys came crawling out of trees and bushes, one boy came forward out of the group and looked like he was going to say something, but I interrupted him.

Now, I'm not normally one to ask for help. In fact, I hate asking for help ever since that step monster yelled at me when I needed help with a bullying situation at school. But in my defense, I was in a pitiful situation and I would never admit it, but I needed help.

"Do you live around here? Is there somewhere I can go? I really need help." I wanted to punch myself for whimpering to these random people, but I didn't. I'm pretty sure that if I punched my own face after asking for help, these people would think I had lost my marbles. That probably wouldn't be very reassuring to them, and they would turn me down.

The leading boy smirked and he raised his club. The others withdrew various weapons and they began to close in on me.

Well, crap.

Time to put 9 years of theater classes to use. With ease, I made my best terrified expression as I began to plot a way out. I'm not a fighter and I never was. Instead, I am a manipulator, I trick people. I get inside people's brain and I can fool anyone, mess with anybody's head. Now, I needed to use that since running was completely out of the question. I always got C's in P.E, but I could pretend to be on their side just long enough for me to hit one of them and run. All I had to do was let them come in around me and bind my hands. That may make it harder, but I wasn't about to give up with my life on the line.

The lead boy approached and looked me up and down before saying, "You're a girl." I desperately wanted to say something like, "Really? I didn't know that! Thanks!" But I had to keep faking. I simply nodded and began crying. That's right- I can cry on command. It can really come in handy. Go me! (Mental self-high-five)!

I can tell that crying ticked the boy off- not exactly what I had in mind. He looked at me like I was a weak little girl. It irked me. A lot.

Two boys seized me by my arms and dragged me into the woods. My feet slid along the dirt, my arms ached from where they were pulling me, but I had to do this. To keep up my act, I kept begging for them to let me go, and hated every bit of it. Ah, the struggles of a prisoner.

"Come on, please! Please don't do this!" I begged, shaking my body in feeble attempts to get away.

"Shut up," one commanded.

I never did take well to orders.

I finally hit the two boys, who promptly collapsed. (Mental self-high-five number two. Go Abby!) I ran fast and I ran far. I was pretty proud of myself, actually, I war running well for being in skinny jeans and wearing boots- just saying.

But, as always, bad luck wasn't far behind. As soon as I had picked up a lot of momentum, I crashed into a boy with piercing greens eyes, just in time to black out.

#3 Bound

When I woke up from my embarrassing black out, I found myself in a cage, bound hand and foot. I had a giant knot on my head that hurt like the dickens, and my legs were sore. The struggle is real.

In case you haven't figured it out yet, I'm not very lucky. It doesn't matter how many bowls of Lucky Charms I would eat in the mornings back at home, fortune never found me. And I mean never. I know, I know, never say never (which is very confusing, since people that say that say never twice in that phrase) but I mean it. One time, I was in English and my teacher told the class that whoever got 100% on the pop quiz could have a chocolate bar. So, I took it and aced it. I know, that sounds lucky, right? Wrong. When the kids lined up to get their chocolate bars, I was the only one that didn't get one because my idiot teacher ran out. Or there was that time that I was suntanning at the beach and some lady brought her dog, even though they weren't allowed, and it peed on me. Twice, when I was standing at the bus stop, cars peeled by after it rained and sprayed me with water. I've sat in wet paint, locked my keys in my car, and spilled hot coffee on

14 INES RUE

myself. But this is by far the most unlucky circumstance I have ever been in.

My luck got worse as the boy with the sharp green eyes came over to the cage (why exactly am I in a cage anyway? Don't hooligans tie people to trees in the movies?) I looked into his eyes intently and recognized them. I had the same exact ones, except ocean blue. Wait, that sounded weird. We don't share eyeballs, but the look in his eyes was one that we shared. Both of our eyes revealed were alert, intelligent, cunning, manipulative, and dangerous. They were the kind of eyes that their owner could control perfectly. We could communicate in eye contact, express everything we felt, or reveal nothing. I wasn't used to being around a person that had the same kind of power I did. It was unnerving.

As he approached the cage, I made my face blank and cold. If he was to interrogate me, I had to make sure he knew nothing. As someone that manipulated like he did, I knew that any information could be a weapon of undoing. Then again, if he was anything like me, the act probably wouldn't work, as I can see right through people. But I couldn't tell anything much about him as he drew closer and knelt at the bars.

He smirked at me. "You're awake."

I rolled my eyes with disdain. "Really? I couldn't tell."

His mood shifted, I could feel it. He had gone from a mocking attitude to a deadly one. A fire seemed to light in him as he snarled, "No one back talks to me."

THAT VOICE INSIDE MY HEAD 15

No one talks back to him? Clearly he was the leader around here. If there was anyone whose bad side I wanted to avoid, it was his. So much for first impressions.

I can always tell when it's a losing battle. This was one of those battles. My next best move was to seal myself up so he couldn't get anymore information. "Yes, sir." I simply said, even if he was my age. He seemed satisfied with my response and- thank the lord on high- he left.

I looked around the camp. It was all boys and they were dancing around a great fire, celebrating. Probably celebrating my capture. Great. They're wild people. Then the boy with green eyes picked up a small pipe and began to play. It was soothing, flowing. I liked it. But I didn't like not knowing what to call the boy. Did random people in the woods have names? I decided on Robbie, it suited him. I watched Robbie play, keeping a close eye on all that happened.

The night wore on with the same hollow music echoing in my ears, the air smelling like wood smoke and the forest as it blew past, the dark closing in around the camp and blanketing this distant world in inky blackness.

Eventually, the boys all went to bed. I didn't feel safe, so I stayed up. Later, I heard the blonde boy who first approached me in the woods call Robbie by the name of Pan. So, Pan it is. Then Pan called the blonde boy Felix.

Hey, I wasn't eavesdropping! I just... pick stuff up! Who am I kidding, I was eavesdropping. That's besides the point. I needed to use all the talents I had if I was going to get out of here alive.

16   INES RUE

Speaking of getting out of here, to escape, I need out of this cage. There was a rock beside the cage that I was able to reach out and grab. Ramming it against the bars would be too loud, so I began to rub it against it like a saw. Hours later, I had made a pretty good sized dent, but it was no use.

After the rock, I started leaning against the side and ramming my shoulder into the cage to make it roll on it's side. Painfully, but efficiently, I was able to roll pretty far and get my hands on a small pocket knife, which I tried to use to cut myself out, but it was no use. The blade was so dull by the end that it was completely useless. You couldn't even scratch a person with it, so I tossed it back out of the cage.

I attempted escape multiple more times but it was no use. I was stuck and these creeps were probably going to eat me. How could life get any better?

#4 Fighting Felix

What's worse than being forced to fight a crazed Felix while everyone watches? Nothing. Absolutely nothing.

I held my fists out even though I doubted it would do any good. I'm very smart because I was exactly correct.

Luckily I grabbed a vine from the nearby tree and quickly wrapped it around Felix for long enough to stab his shoulder once before he broke out, enraged. He grabbed me and flung me against the tree slowly advancing.

I decided to use what skill I had and started talking about his family. I knew nothing about his family, but it was easy to make him miss them. "Wow. Your family would grieve if they could see you now. You're a heartless monster. No wonder they abandoned you."

I had no idea if they abandoned him, I just know that these children all felt rejected, and decided to use that to my advantage.

He hesitated but kept moving forward. The lost boys (that's what Pan keeps calling them) fell silent and listened intently. I could feel Pan's eyes burning into me from one of the trees, but I didn't divert my attention from Felix.

"They hated you, didn't they. Of course, they did. Who could love something like you?" Referring to someone as a thing can make a big impact. "If you ever went back... What would they even say to a villain like you? They wouldn't want you."

I could tell that Felix's family was a VERY touchy subject, I hit the nail on the head. But I seemed to make Felix a lot more angry than sad or weak and he ran at me, driving the knife into my side and I collapsed as he smirked, walking away.

The lost boys whooped and hollered as Felix walked away. I felt two arms lift me and throw me into my cage, the knife smashing the bars, digging it deeper. I was shaking uncontrollably as the world... Got... Fuzzy...

#5 One of the Same

So I woke up after passing out, again and I am crazy angry at myself for fainting. I sat up and jumped when I saw a pair of green eyes peering at me through the bars. Pan regarded me before saying, "That was a good idea- you know, talking about Felix's family. Where did you learn that from?" I just looked at him, refusing to answer. He grabbed the cage and shook it like a maniac, throwing me around and increasing the pain in my side. "I ASKED YOU A QUESTION!" Pan shouted. I sighed. "I taught myself." It was a brief but honest response. He nodded before opening the door. I eyed him suspiciously and then regarded the door. I could run, but my injury would make my capture very easy. That wouldn't work, I could stay put, after all- this may be a test.I decided to take my chances and climbed out. Pan grabbed my arm before I could go anywhere and examined my wound before ripping the dagger out. I screamed but he covered my mouth so thankfully no one heard. He healed the wound with some sort of magic. I should have been shocked, but after the past few days, this was nothing strange. Then he threw me back into the tiny bamboo cage. He sat I front of it and began talking. "All my lost boys fight with their bodies, never have I seen one fight with their mind. That was impressive." I gazed long and hard at him. Where was this going?"We're very similar, Abigail. The mind can be even more powerful than physical strength. Anyway. I want you to become a lost boy, or girl." There it was! I knew he wanted something. "No." I simply replied.He threw open the door and dragged me out by my shirt collar. "You WILL do as I wish or there WILL be consequences." He hollered before once again, returning me to my cage and locking the door, but this time he left.Well that was a lot to take in.

#6 Lost

One month laterI have learned how to handle myself around Pan, and yes I became a lost girl, but it wasn't my choice. I would have preferred to go home, but of course that was not an option. Now a days I just sit around and am forced to do Pan's dirty work. By dirty work, I mean tricking people, luring new lost boys, and convincing the new lost boys that it was safe and then betraying them. Like I said, not my choice but Pan is powerful and I know when I am fighting a losing battle. I honestly discovered in this past month how lost I really am. I sit and wish it was different but that never changes the way things are. I gave up on escaping and fighting back a long time ago when I realized how dangerous this place is. Luckily for me, so am I, so I am not quite as pathetically helpless as I could have been. Pan talks to me a lot. I'm not sure why he keeps me on the island, other than I'm useful to play mind games with people so that he isn't the only one doing so. But I do know one thing. I really am a lost, lost girl.

#7 Truth, Dare, or Die

Truth, dare, or die. Not exactly the name that you recognize. It's exactly what it sounds like. You pick either truth or dare and if you chicken or Pan detects you are lying, you die. Simple rules, really. The boys play this game every other night and it normally gets extreme. I get to play tonight for the first time, as it is normally the boys that play. I sat down on a log and felt the heat of the fire on my face. The boys circled around it on logs, on the ground, in trees, and in the door ways of their tents- filling the camp. Pan stood up. "Alright boys! Let's play!" All the boys cheered and Pan sat down on another log across the fire from me. Everyone hushed and Pan threw a rock in the air, and it ended up knocking Toodles on the head, indicating that he was first to ask someone truth or dare. Toodles turned to Slightly. "Slightly. Truth or dare?" Slightly straightened his shoulders. "Dare." Everyone smiled and glanced around. Toodles gave the worst dares. I bit my lip, worried for Slightly, who was a softie- at least compared to the other boys. Toodles rubbed his hands together and leaned into the fire. " I dare you to go walk past where the fairies live. Naked. Singing Old McDonald had a farm."

THAT VOICE INSIDE MY HEAD   23

The onlookers, including myself erupted into crazy fits in laughter. Slightly turned bright red but he nodded causing the laughter to get two times louder. Slightly stripped and walked into the forest, a group of boys following to make sure he completed the dare. In the meantime the boys would bet on whether he would chicken or not. Slightly came back blushing like nuts the group of boys laughing behind him shouting, "He did it, he did it!" Slightly yanked on his clothes and sat down in his spot. "My turn. Um... Nibs. Truth or dare?" "Truth!" Nibs shouted from one of the trees circling the fire. Toodles gave the crazy dares and Slightly always gave terrible truths. "Tell us. If you had to kiss any BOY here, who would it be?" Asked Slightly, smirking at his cleverness. "Um... I um- I guess Cubby." As Nibs answered, all eyes flicked between Cubby and Nibs. Nibs was red as a baboons butt and Cubby was laughing so hard he fell out of his tree. A few more truths and dares floated around until it was once again Toodles who gave a dare."How about Abigail. Truth, or dare?" My heart stopped. I would be tortured in a million possible ways if I chose dare and truth would make me seem weak. I did NOT want to be weak, so I let my stubbornness get the best of me. "Dare." Everyone fell silent. Everyone was staring at me. NOBODY accepts a dare from Toodles or a truth from Slightly on their first time playing. But I just did. "Really? Wow. Well I am going to hit two birds with one stone..." Toodles had this crazy look in his eye and a dangerous smile on his lips. I was in for it. "Abigail, I dare you to go into Pan's tent with him and you two make out for ten minutes." Everyone's jaws dropped. Slightly froze. Nibs froze. Felix froze. Cubby froze. Marbles froze.

24

INES RUE

All the other 110 lost boys froze. I froze. Most of all, Pan froze. I didn't know what to do. I couldn't do that! So what should I do? "If you refuse you die. It's the rules." Toodles reminded me. I clenched my jaw and stormed into Pan's tent. I heard him say something to Toodles about kicking his BEEP! later on, before he came in. I was sitting in the corner cross apple sauce with my chin rested on my palm. "Look Abigail, most people don't get a dare as extreme as this, but there are rules set and I don't think you want to be thrown in the fire." Said Pan standing in front of me. "We may as well try to make the best of it." He offered his hand to help me up but I stood on my own. "I don't want to. You make me do terrible things and I refuse to so much as touch YOU." I responded plainly. "We don't have a choice." Pan stated. I heard Toodles shout from outside, "The timer doesn't start until the first kiss!" I scowled at the door in the direction his voice came from then turned back to Pan who slammed his lips into mine, surprising me. But since it was this or burn in a fire, I kissed back. Pan moved so that I was walking backwards and wrapped my legs around his waist. It got heated from there. After those 10 minutes we heard Toodles tell, "There's the ten minute mark! You two can be done!" I sprang from the him in seconds. In the broken mirror I could see that my hair was ruined and I was pink and sweaty. I fingered combed my hair and threw it in a high pony tail before returning to my spot on the log. Something had happened in there. I had found myself enjoying it, and more importantly- Pan. I hadn't hated it or him! Why? I have no idea. I am not going to stress over it now. Truth, dare or die continued and only one person was burned alive! One!

THAT VOICE INSIDE MY HEAD   25

That's the fewest there's ever been! The night held some crazy dares. Felix had to eat poop, Dustin had to hang upside down for a tree and sing zippy de do dah in a high voice for three minutes, and Devin had to kiss Toodles. And that was the night I played truth, dare, or die.

#8 The Smallest Spark

Ever since that night of truth, dare, or die Pan had been avoiding me. It's clear why, I mean it's understandable how awkward it is for him. It's awkward for me too. Not that I'm complaining! Pan hasn't sent me to do anything brutal when I would rather sleep in so that's a plus. Felix commonly teases me about the whole thing. We have gotten closer now that he has made an effort to notice I exist. But how could he not? I mean, he's Pan's right hand boy and after that night of course there is now a tie between Pan, him, and I. Most mornings after I wake up I go down to a small cave in the woods to shower in privacy and think. Pan doesn't notice when I'm gone, which is good. No, that's a lie. He knows EVERYTHING about this island so he knows but he doesn't care too much. Where would I go anyway? I have a hideout at the cave that consists of a small bed, a tiny toilet, mini sink, the waterfall/shower, and a small shelf that holds many things. Mainly those things are food, fun objects, resources, weapons, and little treasures I find around camp and Neverland. I also have a notebook there that I write EVERYTHING in. It mainly consists of my conflicted feelings towards Pan. Don't get me wrong, I would still jump at the chance to kill him and run- but now I have to sort some stuff out. I cannot let my emotions get the best of me. They normally do and when the do- I lose all control. I am there, aware of everything but my body is not my own and I do terrible things to people I love without a choice. It's a terrible feeling. It was early one morning that I sat in this cave that I have begun to call The Escape and thought about myself, Pan, and emotion itself. Me caring for Pan was stupid and ridiculous but I couldn't help but question it. Could I actually want him to maybe not die? Like, it's not like I wanted to give him the world or give him stuff or something. But maybe I was beginning to want him to not be dead and coated in his own blood. It wasn't much, nothing to place your money on- but it was a valid thought. It was almost nothing, so dim you could almost never see it, but it was there. The smallest spark.

#9 Thief

I walked through the forest pushing large leaves out of the way and stumbling over branches on the ground. I arrived at my destination about 30 mins away from camp- The Escape. I inhaled deeply, feeling the familiar cool air and smelling the water, hearing it trickle over the rocks. I stepped through the cave entrance and the smell of the cave washed over me as well. I slid off my clothes and stepped into the waterfall letting the cool water drench me and slide down my face. As I scrubbed my body, I heard a noise from the back of the cave. I stepped out of the waterfall and crept along the wall, investigating the strange sound. I peeked around the corner seeing Pan sitting on the bed... Reading my diary! I ducked back and tiptoed towards my towel. I grabbed it and wrapped it tight around my body. I then entered the room and acted surprised when I saw Pan. "Pan?! What are you doing here! Get out! And give me that!" I shouted reaching for my diary. Pan jumped away and opened to my latest entry. "I'm not sure what to do next. I hate him I love him I hate that I love him and it's driving me crazy. Ever since that night I'm not sure. Shouldn't I have been wishing for death to take me the whole time? But I didn't! Why? I can't honestly be falling for him, I mean he's holding me prisoner and could kill me at any second. I don't know what to do. Maybe I could escape. But how? I'm on Neverland and even if I do make it out, Neverland is a star. I will plummet and die. I could hide in the island but Pan can sense EVERYTHING so that's ruled out. I could continue at camp but now that I can't even trust my own emotions I don't know if that would work out-" "Give it back!" I lunged but Pan chuckled and lifted the diary high in the air where I couldn't reach. I had always been short. Curse my height! "No way, this is fun!" He laughed.I felt my face burn, knowing I was blushing like nobody's business and he continued to read the diary. "Half the time I could run up and kiss him, the other half I could stab him. Is this normal? Like I know that sometimes people can't decide on something but this is just nuts. Love, Abigail." He concluded.I shivered when he put love and my name together, but I quickly tackled him and took the diary. "Your horrible!" I screeched.He cracked a taunting smile. "Is this one of those time you want to stab me? Or kiss me?" He sent a burst I magic forward, freezing me in place. He plucked the diary right from my hand and stalked off calling behind him, "It'll wear off in 5 minutes!" Then he took off running into the forest.Five minutes later I unfroze and yanked on my clothes, running in the direction he disappeared in. Where was that little thief? I was going to snap his neck- "Looking for this?" Said a taunting voice that belonged to the dreaded boy sitting in a tree. I growled and began climbing up. I leapt and grabbed it before shimmying down and taking off running. "Isn't this fun?"

He had materialized in front of me and shoved me against a tree. His hands were placed on either side of my head, his lips about 6 inches from mine. He had a dagger strapped to his waist, the cool metal side of the dagger against the skin on my inner thigh. I felt my breathing quicken, he looked like... a sexy demon. He watched me intently. As soon as I noticed that I made it well hidden but thoughts of that night were running through my head. "Is this one of those times you want to kiss me?" He asked smirking."In your dreams. Move." I snapped. He didn't though, stubborn boy that he is. I wanted to kiss him, feel him against me, our skin to touch again so badly!He smirked the biggest smirk that ever smirked. "Oh Abigail, don't you know?" He leaned in close and whispered in my ear, "I can read minds..." With that, he smashed his lip so to mine, still pinning me to the tree. His fingers were laced in mine, holding my hands above my head. I kissed back. He brought his hands down and put them on my waist, pulling me closer. I slid my fingers through his hair and with with a poof of smoke we appeared in his tent, never breaking the kiss. It continued on getting more passionate by the second.

#10- Psycho

It's official. Im absolutely insane! I have lost my marbles! I wonder where they went, maybe they joined the lost boys! I am telling you, I'm psycho. Don't believe me? I kissed Pan, I think I may love the enemy, I let my enemy read through a book of my fricking emotions, and as if that isn't enough- we had a 5 minute make out session. That just takes the cake!So yes, I'm crazy. But as if I didn't have enough problems, I have to worry about what PAN feels too! I definitely got myself into a mess. Why do I have to have creepy stuff like feelings? Bleck! Feelings cloud my judgement! I want them gone. But that's not an option so I have to figure out all this crap.It's not like I would give my life for him! I mean I hardly have known him, since I have only known him a year. What? My trust in next to impossible to gain and you can lose it SO easily. And when i say next to impossible, I mean it. I don't even trust my own parents! But that logical since they...Never mind. The point is that Pan and I have... something. What is it? I don't know. When will it stop? I couldn't say. What's it doing here? I haven't the faintest idea. Why? Absolutely positively no clue.So that's my complicated life. So let's talk about other complications in Neverland! Felix is really sick right now and can't train me. So that means PAN TRAINS ME! Do you know how terrible this is? No, you don't because you have never had a guy you want to kiss and yet strangle train you and see his muscles flex and that makes your knees weak and then he ends up pinning you down because of your weakness so then you want to stab him.Anyway, back to Felix. He got some sort of disease that some bug carried. I am beginning to learn a lot about Neverland, but I'm no Einstein. Pan is though, and it makes me want to stab him. Then he yanks my hand away from what apparently is a deadly plant and I want to kiss him. I am getting so side tracked! This bug is called a neverlife bug. The name is just as menacing as the bug. It has this thing about it that attracts germs and bacteria and when it bites something it moves some of that gross germ collection to the victim. Now Felix is rambling about unicorns and laying in bed just laughing like an idiot. Felix was stressing Pan out because he doesn't want anyone else to get bitten because they would be resting for a week after the bite. Trust me, a stressed Pan is no fun for anyone. He hasn't teased me about the journal ONCE since Felix was bitten. Since Felix used to be the second in command, Pan needed someone to fill in. And can you guess who he chose? Your truly, Abigail Smith! And that made the tension so much better! (Note my sarcasm.) So now Pan and I scheme together. It's fun and he says I'm good at it. I hope so!All these thoughts were steaming through my head as I sat in The Escape as stated at the waterfall. Of course, the demon himself had to interrupt me!"Hey Abigail." The Peter Pan sat next to me. Isn't this just dandy? (Sarcasm again.)

THAT VOICE INSIDE MY HEAD

"What do you want Pan?" I asked, sighing.Pan smiled a little. Oh great. "Peter. My first name is Peter." I rolled my eyes. "No! I thought it was Veronica!" I sighed again, "no duh your name is Peter." Pa- I mean Peter just regarded me before flying his eyes to the waterfall again. "Abigail-""Abby." I interrupted. I had no idea why I just did that. I only let one person- my best friend call me Abby. There it is again! I'm losing my mind!Peter smirked and then continued. "I will give you plenty of time to sort it all out, but when you do- tell me.""Uh... sort what out." I asked, playing dumb."You know EX-ACTLY what."And with that brief conversation, he turned, stood, and teleported away.Great! I really am psycho!

#11 Test

"I- I- I got it sorted out. I figured it all out and I think..." I began, stammering, trying to get the words out. But those words were just running away as I tried to say them. "I think that I um, love you..." I squeezed my eyes shut, terrified that he would hurt me. He will, it's just a matter of time, I was sure of that. Peter didn't do anything for about ten seconds. But then he said, "I like you too." I opened my eyes and looked deep into his through my long eyelashes. He wasn't lying. But he said like, not love. I had been trying for the longest time to stop loving everyone after... The incident. But here I was saying 'I love you', words that haven't left my mouth in 7 years. I hated myself, wanted to kill myself for telling him that. He was my captor, and I just showed him weakness. He could make me painfully suffer using that weakness.Peter smiled and walked away. I wanted to cry, and I knew I was going to. But crying is weakness, so I turned and ran into the forest. Peter had shouted after me, asking what I was doing and to come back. I didn't listen I knew he was behind me, running but I just ran faster I ran as far as I could (which if you had ever seen me run isn't that impressive) I may not be the best at endurance, but I was

THAT VOICE INSIDE MY HEAD   35

very fast. Peter was still behind me, so I dove beneath a tree, quickly formulating a plan. He was pretty far behind me. The only way I knew he was there was because of his shouts, which I could still barely hear. I quickly made a contraption from some vines and branches. I hid right before he ran into the clearing. He paused, he had heard me so he knew I was here."Abby? You can run but you can't hide. I know where you are, this is my island!" He said. He slowly walked towards the bush I had dived into.I yanked a vine next to me just as he stepped into the correct spot. Some vines shot down and grasped him under his arms, yanking him into the trees. Another vine shot out and threw itself around him- binding him a thick tree branch. He struggles as more vines came out to secure him."Abby! Let me go! What the heck are you doing?" He asked trying to break the vines. He tried, but it was no use.I stepped out and said nothing. He looked at me but I just ran into the woods. I finally couldn't do it. I collapsed under a tree and the tears fell. I couldn't do it, I just couldn't do it! I bet Peter was going to use that against me, to hurt me. And it was my fault! The tear came harder and harder until I couldn't breathe. My chest heaved and I felt light headed. Everything hurt."Abby?" Peter entered the clearing, his face shocked at my state. My tears fell harmed we and my breathing was practically nonexistent. Why? Why did this always have to happen. It makes death sound like fun.Peter sat down and wrapped his strong arms around me, pulling me closer until we practically molded into one person. He stroked my hair and murmured quietly into my ear until I stopped crying and let oxygen reach my lungs.It surprised me that Peter was cared even the slightest bit. He looked at my eyes. "Abby? What happened?"I couldn't tell him. I wasn't ready. "N- nothing!" He didn't buy it. I didn't expect him to. He just looked at me like he understood why I didn't want to tell him or why I was bawling in the middle of Neverland. It scared me to find out which one.He got up and I stood next to him. The fact that I had tied him to the tree crossed my mind. "I thought I tied you to the tree branch!" I said, more of a question than a statement."You did." Was all he said in response but I already figured out that he used magic. It wasn't hard. He grabbed my wrist and gently yanked me forward as if exasperated that I was being so weak yet understanding that I was weak and vulnerable. I followed. We arrived at camp and he made sure the lost boys didn't see my red eyes or downcast face. I knew why. He always abused the lost boys when they were crying. I don't blame him- they were weak! But I guess he didn't want to harm me further.He took me into the fighting area and made the lost boys scram. Then he turned towards me and sent a flying kick at my gut. It hit and I fell back, crying out. Guess he did want to torture me. "Get up." Was all he said. I knew I couldn't fight back, I needed to outsmart him. But at the moment my brain was foggy and tears began to fall again. I hated myself for showing weakness which made me cry harder which made Peter harm me more which made me cry more which made me hate myself which made me cry more and- it's a vicious cycle. I gazed at him after about five minutes of this. I just sat there in the dust, knowing it would lose the fight. But I had to ask a stupid question, "Why are you hurting me, Peter?" He looked at me long and hard and just when I thought he would brush off the question to hit me, he answered. "You cried in the forest. That's weak. I don't want you to be weak and we both know that if you are the world will kill you slowly and painfully using that weakness. So I'll make you strong." With that he grabbed a knife and slowly advanced. I understood now. This wasn't a punishment- it was a test. And we all know I always get an A+ on tests.I got up and used the fact that I was fast and slightly flexible to run circles around him and finally disarm him and use it to pin him against a tree. I raised the dagger and aimed for his heart. Just when I was going to hit and saw how scared he was, I dug the knife to the side, pinning his shirt to the tree. "I wouldn't stab you. This was a test, not a challenge." I stated and walked away as Peter struggled to get the knife out of the wood.

#12 Nightmares are Real

It was a year after Peter told me he likes me and now we BOTH say I love you and love each other deeply.

I am now the second in command, bumping Felix down to third. I have every privilege Peter has, and I am in charge of myself. I am basically female Peter. I technically do have to listen to Peter but he never abuses that, thank goodness. We run the camp side by side, and a pair. We have split the lost boys in three. Peter, Felix, and I all train 1/3 of the lost boys, and they are basically our students. We train them, show them the ropes, and make sure they stay in line. When we decide that they don't need a teacher and rule enforcer anymore, we let them take care of themselves and they are an official lost boy.

I train just like Peter. I don't get all compassionate and loving; just because I am a girl. In fact, I'm really mean. I am not afraid to injure a kid and I would never hesitate to give cruel punishments. For example, Nico was misbehaving, so I told my lost boys that they were to all use Nico instead of trees and sacks and targets that day. Nico is barely alive. He would have been dead had I not decided that was enough.

THAT VOICE INSIDE MY HEAD

So, life's pretty good!

Until the nightmares started. Every night I get horrible nightmares of a man dressed in black and red who says a number each night, then stabs Peter to death. Each night the number is smaller. It started at 100, and now it's 73. I have a feeling it's a countdown to Peter's death. But his death won't be natural. That man is going to kill him.

Could he? I don't know, and I don't want to find out.

So I decided I had to leave Neverland. If the man was coming to me in my dreams, he'll hurt Peter through me, since he's already in my head. Peter's best chance is for me to leave.

I began drawing up my plan in the Escape but hid it so Peter wouldn't find it.

This may all seem silly but think about the boys that came here in their dreams just to find that their dream is a nightmare come true! I can't take that chance, not with Peter's life in so much danger.

#13 My Permission

I sat on the beach with my few belongings on a wooden crate, waiting for Hook. I had held a dagger to Hook's throat and forced him to sail me home. Now I just waited.

Smee came forward. "The captain say it's time to board."

"Oh shoot!" I exclaimed, "I realized I let my dagger back there, one second."

I turned back and sprinted into the forest, all the way to camp. The night air made it chilly. I grabbed my favorite dagger and headed back to the ship.

Everyone else had boarded the ship. I was walking across the cool sand when I felt a familiar hand rest on my shoulder. I could smell his beautiful forest smell, but I knew he was not happy. I spun around.

"No one leaves this island without my permission." He said.

"Well I am." I replied and flipped him over my shoulder. He fell to the ground with a thud but got up.

"Abby, this is not a fight that you can win. Don't try. Come back to camp." He was so inviting that I wanted to go. But I knew what he was doing.

THAT VOICE INSIDE MY HEAD   41

"No. You are using magic to make what you say appealing. When I get back you have the authority to punish me, technically." I replied, walking backwards towards the ocean. The sand sank between my toes, scratchy but nice. I wanted to stay in Neverland forever, but I had to go. I have to protect Peter.

I turned and ran up the gangplank and onto the ship. Hook had the shadow trapped, so we were all ready to go.

He put the shadow in the sail and we lifted. I ran to the rail and looked down at the beach. I saw Peter there, looking surprised and heartbroken. I didn't want to leave him, I love him! But that man in my dreams... The number is 23 now. I have to get as far away from Peter as possible. The dream has gotten worse: it used to be just the number and then he stabbed Peter to death. But it was short and blurry. Now it's clearer and longer. I noticed that it is the same dagger every time. It's got a wavy metal blade with engravings of vines on it and a name. I can barely read the name, but I think it says Richard Skin. That is probably the name of the person that wants to kill Peter.

I gazed down at him. "Goodbye." I whispered down at his tear stained face, tears beginning to fall from my eyes as well.

Peter crying was the last thing I saw before Neverland vanished and a town unfolded below.

#14 Math Class

5 months. It's been 5 months since I last saw Peter. I got adopted by the worst family ever and attend school at Gates High School. Gates is the "problem school." As is drug deals in the hallways, guns in people's lockers, and just the most crappy people you could ever imagine. So that's my new school.

I was currently sitting in third period math class doing my work. I was just solving problem 37 when I felt an unsettling breeze. I glanced around at the idiots at my table, but they didn't notice. I looked down at my paper and shook my head, clearing my thoughts. I gazed at the doodles on the side of the work page. Pan's pipes, the camp fire, Peter's eyes, a mermaid tail, Neverland, the list goes on. So yes, I miss home. And yes, I want to go back. The number in my dreams already reached zero. On the last night I heard Peter scream in agony at the blows. That was the only time he did that. I hope Peter is safe, but knowing my luck, he's not. I'll bet he's dead.

I was halfway through problem 38 when I felt a hand on my shoulder. I turned around slowly, but no one was there. The hand moved away.

THAT VOICE INSIDE MY HEAD

The smell of damp forest and wood smoke wafted up to my nose. That's when I figured it out. Peter.

"Peter?" I whispered.

He didn't respond. I doubted he would. But I knew he was there. I could feel it. He was next to me. I shut the notebook and began to quietly put all my things away in my backpack.

I walked up to the desk. "Mr. Green?"

"Hmm?" Answered my math teacher, looking up from his book.

"May I use the restroom?" I asked, acting like it was an emergency. He rolled his eyes. "Fine."

I turned on my heel and left the room quickly. I approached the bathroom and ducked inside the largest stall.

"Peter? Are you still there?" My voice echoed in the empty restroom.

"Yes."

I almost broke down right there. Hearing his voice after 5 months just... I didn't have the words to describe it.

The air in front of me rippled and he came into view.

I just stood there. I stared into his piercing eyes and at his face. It has been so long since I had seen his face...

He stared back at me.

Then I did something embarrassing. I broke down crying. The tears just kept flowing. I couldn't believe that he was alive, when I was so certain he was dead. I cried and cried. I simply couldn't bear it.

Peter ran closer and yanked me into a hug. "Sh. Calm down, love."

Hearing his voice broke me even more. I could feel everything falling down. I kept crying and couldn't stop.

He held me and he began to let loose some tears of his own.

I was able to get a gasp of breath. "I'm sorry! I didn't mean it, I didn't want to leave Neverland! But... Rumplestiltskin! He... He was going t- to kill you and I just couldn't let him and so I had to get far away and I- and I-"

"I know. It's okay, Abby." He said gently.

I looked up into his eyes.

"Thank you, Peter. Gosh, that was embarrassing! Don't tell anyone." I said, slightly laughing.

I felt like a bajillion pounds had been taken off of me. It was like breaking the surface of the water and getting a breath of air. It was like that feeling when you get away with it. It was total and complete relief.

I broke into the biggest smile, looking at Peter and knowing it was alright.

Then I heard something in the other stall. It was the sound of a blade being drawn. Then I heard a faint tick... Tick... Tick...

"HIT THE DECK!" I yelled slamming into the floor behind the toilet, dragging Peter behind me. Just as the walls between the stalls exploded.

#15 Enemies on Earth

The explosion rattled the building and kids ran screaming from the school. The teachers panicked, grabbed their coffee, and ran after the students.

My body had taken the majority of the force, making my breathing rugged and my muscles scream.

I was able to squint through the rubble, and make out the shape of one of my earthly enemies, Margaret Lex. Margaret had always been a jerk after her boyfriend developed eyes for me. I never had any sort of connection with her boyfriend, but that didn't matter to Margaret. She was a viper hidden inside human flesh. I hated her guts. And she wanted me dead.

Margaret always was the best in science. I should have known she would assemble a bomb of some sorts.

I looked over at Peter. He was fine, peering into the room at Margaret. "W- who?" He asked.

"Later." I replied, quick and to the point.

Peter and I stood. We readied our fists, preparing for a fight, but Margaret ran off. We ran out of the bathroom and through the long school hallways. I burst through a door and yanked Peter out. The police had arrived and began running inside.

"Neverland." That was explanation enough. Peter nodded and reached for the vile of pixie dust around his neck. He panicked and I knew something was very wrong.

I stared at him, not really wanting him to answer, but asked, "The explosion destroyed it, didn't it."

Peter's expression gave me plenty of confirmation.

I grabbed his wrist and yanked him forwards, beginning to run down the street. We ran a few blocks then dove into an alley to catch our breath. I leaned against the cold stone wall and slid down it, resting on the ground. Peter sat next to me.

"Who was that? And... How did she have a bomb?" He asked, a dangerous glint in his eyes.

"Margaret Williams. She's been after me ever since I attracted the attention of her boyfriend. As to how she got a bomb... She was always really good in science, particularly chemistry, so she probably made it." I leaned into his shoulder. "Peter? How in the world are we going to get home?"

"Slow down. You attracted another guy's attention?" I could sense a threatening anger rising up in his voice.

I lifted my head from his shoulder. "Yeah, he thought I was hot. I turned him down."

Peter raised his eyebrows. "You waited for me? Although I don't blame you." He flexed and smirked at me.

THAT VOICE INSIDE MY HEAD 47

I rolled my eyes. "In case you hadn't noticed I never thought I would see you, ever again. So no, it was just still grieving."

"Yeah, sure you were." His smirk got bigger.

"I was!" I insisted, indignantly. It was true, I had been broken-hearted and dating another guy? That wasn't happening.

Peter chuckled and wrapped me in a hug. "Whatever."

I glared at him.

"Rest. I know a place with magic that we can go to. We'll open a portal there, or see if they have pixie dust. Then we can go home. But it's in Maine, and we're in Indiana. Right?" He asked, quizzically.

"Yeah. Indiana. Corn and beans for miles and miles with literally nothing to do. Nothing. So yes, we're in Indiana." I replied, annoyed at the state an it's dumb agriculture.

He chuckled. "Then yeah. You'll need your sleep. Night."

"No."

He looked confused. "What? Abby, you need rest to-"

"And I'll get it."

He looked at me like I had lost my marbles. "Uh, Abby. If you aren't sleeping, you aren't getting any sleep." He spoke in the tone you would use with a three year old.

"I'll sleep," I explained, "but I'm taking first watch."

"Abby please just rest-"

"No, Peter."

We had a staring contest, and I won.

"Ugh. Fine. Night. Wake me halfway through the night, okay?" He said grudgingly.

I nodded and smirked as he lay down, finally accepting that I won.

I leaned my head back against the stone and thought about him. I couldn't believe I had him back. I mean, I thought... I thought he was dead. I wasn't sure that this was even real. This was probably an illusion, to give me something good and then rip it away.

I needed to understand what those dreams meant, though. And I needed to know what happened when Rumplestiltskin attacked. Plus I needed to know how we were going to get back. I was lacking a lot of valuable information.

#16 Deals

Peter awoke the next morning, ticked that I didn't let him take the second watch. We stole two happy meals from McDonalds, "Some kid is in the play place! He's hurt and bleeding!" And then some cash from a convenience store, "There's some kids at the slushy machine drinking out of the spout, sir." Then we hopped on the bus headed to Maine and to Storybrooke. I was currently sitting next to Peter, who kept looking out the window and muttering about not being able to kill the fat man across the aisle who was sleeping. And snoring. And it didn't help that he farted, either. So the bus stunk, there was drool on that man's seat, the lady on the other side of Peter had a cat in a cage on her lap that was yowling, on my other side was some old lady with clammy skin and a breathing problem, and so all this was really angering Peter.

"How did you manage living in this world for so long? This is truly the most cruel torture even I could dream up. I should start using this back at camp. How threatening does "The Bus Treatment" sound?" He asked, shooting death glares at the lady's cat.

50 INES RUE

I smiled, "I don't know about threatening, but it certainly will force anyone to give up information. I would crack pretty fast!"

We smiled at eachother. I was just glad to have him back. He didn't joke much, so I decided I had to seize this moment. I rested my head on his shoulder. He put his arm around me. I lay there for a while before my eyes closed.

A hand stroked my hair. "We're here, Abby."

My eyes fluttered open. I blinked and squeezed my eyes firmly shut at the lights in the bus. I heard a chuckle before I was able to fully see. It takes me longer to get adjusted to light than most people.

I looked around and my eyes fell onto Peter.

Then I noticed that we were the only ones on the bus, besides the driver. "Last stop: Storybrooke, Maine. Dunno why you kids would travel here of all places, but 'ere ya go!"

I sat up and Peter slid out before grabbing my hand and taking me off the bus into the crisp night air.

My bare right foot stepped onto the cold stone, then the left. The moss felt squishy between my toes. We were right by a forest on a rainy, cold, empty road. The bus pulled away and down the opposite way, headed for civilization. A green sign was slightly lit up from the tail lights of the bus, but then disappeared into the darkness as the bus got far enough away. Luckily, I have great night vision.

"Entering Storybrooke." I read.

Peter nodded. He held out his hand to the road in front of us. "That means my magic should be back." A wet stick on the road flew into

THAT VOICE INSIDE MY HEAD   51

his hand. It immediately dried. His other hand released some sparks and lit the top of the stick, so that we had a torch.

I inched away from him.

He looked over at me. "Why are you moving away? You're not scared of fire, you dance around it with me all the time. You've seen magic, in fact, Neverland has started to use it's magic to assist you. What's wrong?"

I shrugged. "Just strange to see magic in this world." This was true, and I could tell that Peter used more magic to determine if I was truthful. He nodded and accepted it.

I went back over to him and we stared out at the wet pavement. The water dripped down my face and began forming beads of water in my hair like a pearl veil. Peter noticed. He smiled and grasped my hand firmly, beginning to walk down the street.

The torch shone out in the night, cutting through the dark.

"Why do we need a torch? Won't that give away our location?" I asked, puzzled.

He shook his head. "We'll put it out when we get close to the town. Then we can sneak along the shadows."

I smiled. I loved hiding in the darkness, waiting to pounce on a victim. I'm like a cat, or something.

Peter and I walked for 15 minutes before he said, "Wait!"

I could feel a rumble in the concrete under our feet. Car.

He was squinting down the road, looking. I grabbed him around the waist with one arm and the torch with the other. I smothered the torch in a puddle of water, and lept towards the forest on the

INES RUE

side of the road at the same time. We rolled into the bushes just as a 1990-1992 Cadillac sped by, driven by an old man in a tux. He had shoulder length gray hair, and a serious expression on his face. He had an aura of power, almost as strong as Peter's. He went down the road and disappeared into the fog. He seemed familiar...

Peter looked upset as we kept walking down the road. Not ten minutes later, I felt that rumble again. I tried to yank Peter into the trees to hide us, but he simply shoved me into the forest. I was startled, not expecting him to shove me so roughly. I fell onto my back into the trees, hidden, and hit my head on a rock. I struggled to my feet, but fell again.

Peter glanced over at the noise. "Stay quiet."

I knew he had some sort of plan and I needed to stay hidden and not him, but I was still wanted to leave. But I knew not to doubt my boyfriend. I stayed there and waited, patiently and silently, clutching my head. I felt some sort of warm liquid on my hand. Blood. Great!

The car shot down the road like a bullet. I was about to run up and shove Peter out of the way, taking the hit myself, but the car halted three inches from him. He stood in The middle of the road, arms crossed, a smirk dancing on his face.

The lights on the car went out and the night plunged into darkness. I could feel the dark magic thickening to the point of suffocation in the air. I wanted to go up and stand beside Peter, but I had a pretty good idea why Peter didn't want me to been seen. If this man connected the dots and discovered that Peter loved me, that would be a way for him to hurt Peter, I'm a weakness.

THAT VOICE INSIDE MY HEAD   53

My pupils dilated and I looked into the darkness. My eyes adjust to the dark really fast. I saw the two stare at each other through the gloom, right in the eyes. Then Peter's gaze intensified. The other man in the car blinked and looked away. He stepped out of the car, shutting the door. He approached Peter and stood, leaning against the front of the car.

"What are you doing here, Papa?" asked the man.

I stopped and looked at the two of them. The man looked incredibly angry, but was doing a pretty good job of covering it up. But I'm good at reading people. Peter had stiffened. His eyes hardened. He didn't want me to hear that.

I was going to have to talk to him about that... but for now, I needed to focus on keeping myself hidden. The shadows seemed to cover me further. I looked down at myself, but there was nothing to see, it was too dark for me to even see my own hand when I held it right in front of my face. Peter was helping me remain hidden. He was also telling me to stay hidden. But that didn't work out.

The man smiled. "You're a long way from your territory, Pan. This here, is mine. Here, I am the one in control. Not you. I know everything that happens, not you. Come here, girl. I know you're there. He looked straight into the shadows making direct eye contact. Peter slowly moved his eyes to where I was, too. His jade eyes softened and he sent a clear message, that little voice inside my head said, "It's pointless. He knows. Come on. I can still protect you."

I glared back at him. "I can protect myself, Peter!"

"I know. Come on." His eyes were worried, now.

54   INES RUE

I stepped out of the shadows, the black melting off of me, but when I emerged it swirled around me, dressing me in a black dress that fell almost to my feet, a black cloak, and a black iron panpipe pendant on a silver chain around my neck that seemed to have some dark magic aura inside it. The mist swirled and mixed with the darkness, creating a sword and dark hilt, attaching to a black belt. My hair was whisked into a braid, tied with a black ribbon. The darkness created some black shoes, that matched the outfit, but where secure enough to run in. Some of the darkness seemed to trail behind me, with me, around me. This was obviously something Peter did. He wanted me to be able to get away if need be. I walked slowly up to Peter and stood beside him, one hand resting on the handle of my sword, ready to fight my way out.

The man spoke. "Well, looky here. My father and, could this be my potential step mother?"

I nearly barfed. Me? A mother? That would require growing up. No.

The man laughed slightly. "Well that's a shame. She's opposed to motherhood. Sorry, Papa, you won't be getting another child to sacrifice for your own good anytime soon."

Huh? I feel like I'm missing something just below the surface...

"You haven't told her, Papa? About your child, your origin, how you were an old man once? No?"

My heart rate increased. But this man sounded just like Peter, the way he would taunt people on Neverland. And when Peter did that, he was preying on their secrets and fears, twisting reality. This man

THAT VOICE INSIDE MY HEAD 55

could be making all this up. I wasn't about to believe him anytime soon.

All of the sudden, I realized why the man looked familiar. He was the man in my dreams that tried to kill Peter, the whole reason I left Neverland! This man must have been tricking me, trying to use me to control Peter, getting me to come down to this world, his world! Rumplestilskin.

I drew my sword, put myself between Peter and Rumplestilskin. I held the sword up perfectly aimed at the man's beating heart.

Peter grabbed my other arm and tried to yank me back, but I lunged away from Peter and attacked The Dark One. He summoned strong dark magic and shot it at me, but I dodged. Peter had help me practice dodging magic before, incase a "hero" with light magic came to Neverland. The spell hit a tree, which promptly burned to ashes.

"STOP!" Peter's voice rang out and the two of us froze, me jumping above Rumpletilskin, about to bring my sword down on his head, him with a fire ball rocketing towards me, but that froze, too. Peter waved his hand and the fire disappeared. Rumplestilskin magically returned to the car in the same position he was in before the fight. I returned to Peter's side, sword put away facing Rumplestiltskin, same as beforehand, except that Peter was slightly in front of me. We unfroze, and Peter's arm shot out in front of me, crossing my body and preventing me from lunging at Rumplestilskin.

"Rumplestilskin." I growled, deep and threatening in my throat. Each letter laced with venom and deep hatred.

He smiled. "Miss Smith."

56 INES RUE

I growled and tried to go forward but Peter gave me that "NO!" look and I drew back.

"Let's get down to business, Rumple. I'm here to make a deal." Said Peter.

Rumplestilskin smiled an insincere smile. "A deal?"

Peter didn't respond, just looked at him.

"What do you want?" Asked Rumple.

Peter smirked. "I'm flexible. Either a magic bean, the Hatter's hat, a Magic Door, Pixiedust, or a Mirror Portal."

Rumplestilskin nodded. "No pixie dust? No way back to Neverland? And I'M the only way back. Well, you are much more useful to me here than in Neverland. I'm not giving you any means of transportation back to Neverland." He paused. "Unless, there is a book I want..."

I stared at him. Despite Peter's warning glance, I piped up. "A book? What book, To Kill a Mockingbird?"

Peter and Rumple looked at me at the same time, "What?"

I shook my head. "What book do you want?"

"Abby," Peter said softly, "I'm making this deal. Stay out of it, I don't want you getting sucked into this."

"Well it's too late for that, dearie."

And in a swirl of purple I ended up in a cage. I was in the back of a shop full of antiques. There was some noise coming from the front of the shop. Did Peter send me here? Or did Rumpelstiltskin?

A Woman entered the room carrying a book, reading. I scooted back into the cage. She looked up from her book and saw me. She

THAT VOICE INSIDE MY HEAD 57

had curly brown hair and blue eyes. She gasped and ran over. She had an australian accent. "What happened to you? Why are you in a cage? Who are you? What's going on? Rumple! I'll get you out, one moment."

She ran over to a shelf and grabbed a crowbar. Why she had a crowbar, I will never know. She tried to open the cage but it shimmered with purple light when she touched it, zapping her. "Ow! Rumple, I told him no more dark magic..."

She ran out of the room, then poked her head back in. "I'll be right back. Do you know where Rumple is?"

"The Dark One?"

She winced.

"Yes. He's on this road down by a sign that says, 'Entering Storybrooke' and he's making a deal with my... friend." I said.

The woman raised her eyebrows at 'Friend' but ran out of the room.

I figured I should let her stop him. She looks the right age to be his daughter.

About half an hour later I heard the door slam and a bell ring. Then I heard the girl arguing with Rumplestiltskin.

"You trapped a teenage girl in a cage that will zap her if she tries to escape!"

"It was for the best, Belle."

Belle. That was her name.

"You said no more magic!"

"I need magic!"

58 INES RUE

"And you were making a deal with her friend! You sent him to his death somewhere, didn't you!"

"If he dies, he deserves it!"

"RUMPLE!"

"Belle, it's whats going to get us our happy ending!"

"By hurting them? There's other ways to get happy endings, Rumple! We don't need dark magic!"

"Belle..."

"NO! I said no more magic, and I mean it. Let that poor girl go, and go bring her friend back!"

"He has to get the payment for me to give him what he needs."

"Why can't you just help him! Be nice!"

Nice. This must mean that the girl, Belle, is a "hero." A villain having a "hero" and a child. Strange! And why did she call him by his first name? maybe she was adopted...

"They're both evil, Belle."

"No, they're not! That girl is terrified and would never hurt a fly!"

So my acting worked... Who's awesome? Abby's awesome? Who's awesome? Abby's awesome!

"Release the girl! And help the boy, no charge!"

"Belle-"

"Do it!"

I heard a sigh and then the two came in. I pretend to look terrified, and started crying. Thats right, I can cry on command. It's handy.

Belle looked at Rumple, clearly angry.

THAT VOICE INSIDE MY HEAD 59

Rumplestiltskin approached the cage and took the spell down, and opened the door. He looked at me with a look that clearly said, "This is not over."

Belle lead me into the main room, where The Dark One summoned some magic and brought Peter into the room. Peter looked around and his eyes fell onto me. I could tell into took a lot for him to not run to me. Rumplestiltskin handed him a pouch. Peter looked inside and then shut it. Belle apologized to us both and then took Rumplestiltskin away. We ran out of the shop and to the clock tower. Peter and I scaled it and then ran, and jumped. He threw a magic bean from inside the pouch down below us and we fell through a swirling green portal, off to Neverland!

Just before we fell through I looked at Peter, "I swear, you'll be the death of me."

He laughed and we fell through into the coldness in the portal...

#17 Home Coming

I opened my eyelids, peering at the trees through my eyelashes.

Peter.

I looked around, trying to spot him. He turned out to be next to me, sprawled on the sand. He sat up and shook his head, flinging sand everywhere.

I tackled him in a hug. "WE DID IT! WE'RE HERE!" I got up and sat back on my haunches. "Oh, Neverland, I missed you!" I grabbed the sand in my hands and let it run through my fingers. It was a warm, scratchy sensation that sent shivers up my spine. I flopped into the sand and the sand legit hugged me.

Before I left, since I was connected to Peter, and he was the Island and Shadow (in a weird magical way), so the shadow and Neverland seemed to love me, too. Their magic came to my aid when I needed it and always tried to help me. Not that I could control it, I have no magic. Shadow and Neverland are free spirits: they just care about me. I'm not sure how that works, but it does.

Peter smiled. "Abby?"

THAT VOICE INSIDE MY HEAD   61

I turned, the sand still grasping at me like it was saying "Welcome! Abby, we missed you!"

"What?" I answered.

"How are you planning to," he paused, "tell the lost boys? I mean, they may be happy you're home, sad you were gone, or even angry that you left."

I nodded. "If they're happy, great. If they're sad, then they need to toughen up, and if they're angry, I can take them."

He grinned. "I like your thinking!"

He stood and offered me his hand. I stood. "Wait!" I cried. "Uh... are we going to camp?"

He looked at me long and hard, as if to determine whether I was trying to say not to go, or I was just stupid. He decided on the first one. Smart boy.

"Yes. You don't want to go? I thought we just-"

"I have something to take care of. Just... tell my family that I'm finally coming home."

He smiled, and I could faintly see moisture in his eyes, happy tears. He nodded and ran camp. I knew what he was thinking. He was crazy happy to have me back, and was glad that Neverland was my home and he and the lost ones were my family.

After he sprinted off, I turned to the woods. "Shadow?"

As I said before, Peter's shadow and I are tight now. Right on time, Shadow swoops down and hugs me. "You're back!"

I nodded. "That I am."

He studied my expression. "Why?"

I rolled my eyes. "Why? That's all you got? Well, I met Peter in the human world, and I realized he was alive and that we needed to get back to Neverland because he was alive so I came back. It was very hard getting here..." I thought about our journey.

Shadow read my thoughts and laughed. "Hard is an understatement. I mean, kidnapped by Pan's s- Rumpelstiltskin. And the way you tricked Belle was pretty good, she's clever. Nice job."

I smirked. "Did you ever have a doubt?"

He shook his head. "No. So, darling, shouldn't you be at camp? The lost boys want to see you! Especially Felix. Pan's been stressed and so Felix wanted you back."

I smiled. "Yeah, I do need to get back. Catch you later, Pop Tart!"

We laughed as I jogged into the woods. Yes, Shadow and I have nicknames for eachother. He's a sliver of Peter, so it's not weird.

I heard whoops and hoots and hollers from camp as I approached, they were celebrating. Probably my arrival. The lost boys hated me, since I was just like Peter. They probably had a lot of false enthusiasm. I entered and immediately, Felix came up to me. "What were you thinking? Do you know how impossible Pan was for the 5 months you were gone!"

I laughed. The party continued on, and no one heard us. "So I've heard, dork."

"What? Who?"

"Shadow."

THAT VOICE INSIDE MY HEAD 63

He nodded, then returned to his angry state. "Do you know how many boys were killed in those 5 months. When you left we had 118 boys. We have 72, now."

I raised my eyebrows. "Wow. Pan's been busy." I always call him Pan when around the lost boys, only Peter when we're alone.

Felix sighed, deflating. "Well, at least you had the sense to come back."

I growled and made sure to subtly swipe my leg underneath his, tripping him as I walked back to Peter.

Peter halts the celebration for my return and announces that I'm back. They cheer and go back to dancing and yelling.

Peter gets out his Pan Pipes. I listen to him play and dance around with the boys. Yeah, I thought of them as family, (ish), but make no mistake, I was not going to turn all mushy and love them. Punishment will still continue, even death. And I will not hesitate to restore order to my third of the boys that Peter, Felix, and I train.

After dancing around the fire, I return to Peter's side and hum along to the pipes. The night wears on and we celebrate until we see the first kiss of sunlight cast it's light on our faces.

Then we went to start the day. We ate breakfast and went to training. I was sad to see that they had really slacked off while I was gone. I worked them until they all passed out. Then they took the rest of the day off. I planned to keep doing this until they are back to where I had them.

I, on the other hand, came back five months older than I was before and in better quality. I had to fight my way out a lot in that school. I never ceased training.

Now, I had troops to deal with.

When the day concluded, I went back to Peter's tent and he played his pipes for me.

I drifted off to sleep and slept like a rock, then woke up and made my third work until they passed out again.

This cycle repeated for about a month and I had primed my lost boys. At this point I talked to Peter about a subject I knew I should tread lightly upon.

"Hey Peter? I was wondering about Rumpletilskin. He called you papa. Why?"

Peter turned rigid and dragged me into the tent. I angrily lashed out and he released me. I plopped down on the bed.

And he told me.

And I died inside.

#18 Served Cold

Cinderella.

That was her name. The mother of Rumplestilskin, princess, and in another world. But I'm clever.

I snuck out of Peter and I's tent. After I learned that he had a child with another woman and just kinda forgot to tell me that the mother was a princess, he was once a 50 year old man, he sacrificed his son, his son turned into the dark one, and then kidnapped me, so I am his step mother really makes me mad. So I had refused to sleep next to him, instead sleeping across the room on the floor.

Peter stirred and lifted his head. "Where...?"

I pretend to still be mad at him, but I had secretly directed my anger at Cinderella. I loved Peter and when I lose control of my emotions, I can really hurt people. So I'd prefer that to be at her than my love.

So I pretend to hate him to get out. "None of your business! Unlike the fact that you had a son was MY business! Jerk!"

He sighed and fell back on the pillow, closing his eyes.

I stormed out and then dropped the act. My feet pound the dirt and I shoot like a bullet towards the ocean. I get there and step into the waves. They should be here any minute now...

As predicted, a mermaid lunged up and grabbed at me, attempting to yank me under. I grabbed her and yanked her on shore, where she couldn't get away.

"Abigail! Word floating around the sea is that you discovered Peter's son and that he had an affair with someone else... How sad. Are you plotting to kill him?" She asked, fake emotion on her face.

I lunged forward and held a dagger to her neck. "Not. Another. Word."

The mermaid bowed her head on submission. I moved the dagger away.

"Just one thing, miss." She asked, looking at me for permission to continue.

I raised my eyebrows, telling her to go on.

"Revenge is a dish best served cold."

I nodded. She was right.

I began to direct her. "Open a portal."

She smiled a dark smile. "I need to know where to, miss."

"Far away, a place called Storybrooke."

#19 Vengance

Vengeance. That's all I wanted. This Cinderella had a child... Peter's child...

According to Peter, she became pregnant and then went to Storybrooke to have her child. She had him, and his future self tried to steal him... I'm getting to that. The child was sent to Peter after that, and Peter cared for him for a while but traded him for becoming Peter Pan (I don't blame him!) and so the child was sent to these women and grew up tough. He married a girl named Melia and had a child, Balefire, with her. Then she left him for Captain Hook, or Killian Jones, but died. Their child left Peter's child (Let's see, this Balefire would be my step grandson. I think. Gee, I don't like thinking about this!) and went to Neverland. He was here for a little while. I arrived shortly after he left. Meanwhile, Peter's child went and became the Dark One, therefore immortal except to the dagger. So when Balefire escaped (a long time later, but Neverland keeps you young) his father was alive as well. This Balefire character had a child, Henry, with a woman named Emma Swan, the savior. Their son also is going to be the one to save magic, once Peter gets him here. Balefire was away for a long time, abandoning Emma at the command of Pinocchio, or August. Meanwhile a curse is in Storybrooke and the Evil Queen remains in control. Emma comes and breaks this curse and Rumplestiltskin (Peter's son) adapts the name Mr. Gold and owns a pawn shop filled with magic. He is still there. Then, since he hated his childhood, he time traveled and tried to steal away himself in a complex time loop from Cinderella, causing the Butterfly effect. Because he tried to destroy his childhood and be someone else, he caused it. It's complicated.

But now he is in that old pawn shop and his mother lives in Storybrooke. And I plan to kill her.

As I reviewed history in my head, I was suddenly interrupted by being thrown into the harbor in Storybrooke by the portal. I swam ashore and snuck behind a building. I couldn't do magic, so I had to do it the hard way. Looking at the building, I realized it was the pawn shop owned by my step son. Ugh...

I slipped in the back door. Not even locked. I snuck into the house portion and grabbed a towel, beginning to dry myself off. I put the towel back and fixed myself so I looked a little less suspicious. I got out quickly, making sure not to leave any trace of my being and went back outside. I walked down the streets of Storybrooke and stopped right where I wanted. The apartment building. I let myself in and went to the apartment of Snow White and Prince Charming. God, they were annoying.

I pushed my ear to the door and then tried the knob. Unlocked. What do you expect from goodie goodies? I went straight to where

THAT VOICE INSIDE MY HEAD

69

they let Emma sleep. I went in and immediately found what I was looking for. A pistol. I replaced it with a fake one that I had (I didn't have a real one!) and was about to leave when I heard voices. I had shut the main door in case someone walked by. I glanced around and dropped to the floor. I peered under the bed. There was just enough room. I squeezed in, pistol at the ready.

The door opened to the apartment. I heard White, Charming, Swan, and Mills. They were laughing and apparently Henry had succeeded at something and they were celebrating. I must have been under the bed, frozen for a few hours because it began to grow dark. It was strange, living where time was nonexistent then having to worry about time.

Eventually, I peeked my head out as they were in the living room. I looked at the clock. 9 pm. All the sudden I heard running coming towards the bedroom and shouts. I ducked back under the bed as Swan grabbed the fake pistol and ran out. I heard a few important words.

"Gold's"

"Break in"

"Wet towel"

Apparently Mr. and Mrs. Gold came back sooner than planned. Oh well. It got the goods out of the apartment so I could get out. Everyone went down there and I snuck to the Laundromat where Cinderella worked. She was about to leave when I blocked the door. We were the only ones around.

I lunged forward and pushed her against the wall. She struggled pitifully and I shoved a sock from the laundry basket in her mouth. She tried to scream but it was no use. I aimed and-

BANG!

The gunshot left a high pitched sound in my ears. Cinderella fell to the ground, dead. That was all the trouble I wanted to cause. I bolted out the backdoor as the crowds ran towards the Laundry Mat. They shouted and pointed. Swan began to sprint full speed towards me. I kicked it into high gear as adrenaline kicked in. She stopped and aimed her gun and fired. But there was no sound as she pulled the trigger on the decoy pistol. I turned and fired the real gun at her leg, hitting my mark perfectly when she started after me. I turned and whirled around, sprinting with all my might towards the harbor where the mermaid waited anxiously. All the sudden, The Dark One materialized in front of me. I crashed into him and he grabbed my wrist, yanking me up again. His cold eyes shone.

"So you're the one that broke into my house, dearie?" He asked in a harsh, taunting manner. I inwardly sighed. Definitely Peter's child.

I laughed. "You'd do well not to threaten your stepmother. Your father might punish you..."

His eyes flashed as he recognised me. "WHERE? WHERE IS PAN?"

I just looked him straight in the eye. White was weeping over Swan's leg along with the Prince Pathetic.

Belle caught up and grabbed Gold's shoulder. "Stop! Don't KILL her!"

THAT VOICE INSIDE MY HEAD 71

I used this distraction to slip out of his grasp and fire two shots, one at Belle, and one at her husband. Then I dove into the water and returned to Neverland.

And a VERY unhappy Peter.

#20- Fury and Resolution

Furious. That's probably the best word to describe Peter Pan as I arrived back on Neverland's soil. He looked as though he was going to split at the seams. His anger seemed to have controlled Neverland as well, because it did not seem to welcome me back. In fact, it seemed to want me gone. Right away.

Peter stormed towards me, grabbed my wrist and yanked me towards his thinking tree.

We arrived, and only then did he speak. "YOU LEFT THE IS-LAND!" He then used some choice words before saying, "AND THEN YOU KILLED HER! YOU KILLED CINDERELLA!"

I rolled my eyes. "When have you ever been upset about murdering someone? Honestly Peter."

"ITS NOT THE FACT THAT SHE'S DEAD THAT I'M AN-GRY ABOUT," I could practically see the heated anger burning inside him while he shouted, "I'M ANGRY THAT YOU LEFT THE," Beep! "ING ISLAND! I SWEAR, ABIGAIL, I SHOULD JUST KILL YOU!"

Oh no... Oh no no no no no!

THAT VOICE INSIDE MY HEAD 73

Though all logic in my head said, "Stop stay put he's just venting, stupid!"

My instincts were screaming, "RUN, STUPID!" And, of course, screams will always drown out the surrounding noise.

I turned and went a mighty three feet (I know, I'm so talented.) before Peter grabbed my arm, roughly, and yanked me backwards. My feet skidded in the dirt and the island was all too happy to trip me. I fell and my back hit first, sending waves of displeasure through my body. Then my head hit a rock and then a painful sensation washed over me. I must have hit hard. There were white spots dancing across my vision. But then I realized I could think. I also couldn't remember much... My name was Alex... Or was it Amanda? But there was one thing I could think: THIS IS NOT GOOD!

A figure loomed over me. This figure grabbed my arms and hoisted me up in it's iron clutches. I could make out eyes... green eyes... But the face was only half formed, the rest was blurry, still. But I saw eyes...

I saw purple smoke. Then felt that I was layed down on something soft. This figure began to talk.

"Abby? Abby? ABBY?" His voice was frantic, and panicked. He was talking to someone... but the name Abby seemed familiar. Where had I heard that?

I felt a burning in my head and neck as a hand passed over me. I felt better and bits and pieces, little thoughts came back to me. I saw some memories, of some Peter guy, was that the figure with me? The figure was coming into focus faster... yes, I think this is Peter. I couldn't remember much about him. I knew that he was on my side, though.

I lay there for five(ish) minutes. By then I remembered everything. I glared up at the concerned devil above me.

"And, you're glaring at me. Remembering, love?" He asked in a caring yet taunting tone.

A large, dramatic sigh escaped my lips. "Yeah."

He smirked. "Look, I'm not angry that you killed Cinderella, although she was an amazing pawn... (His voice became forlorn, but perked up) Okay? Oh, and, um... sorryaboutyourhead!"

I raised an eyebrow. Peter may have sped through the end but I caught that.

"Ok and... I'm sorryforleaving." I imitated

He laughed and offered a hand up. I accepted and he yanked hard and fast so that I ended close to him, standing on the ground in his tent.

He leaned in, giving me a quick kiss before saying, "Come on. We've got troops to train."

"Ugh, don't remind me!" I laughed. We seperated so that our personal space bubbles no longer popped.

I stepped into the sunlight and went over to where my troops were gathered.

#21 Horrible Perfection

Peter and I are horrible. Both of us are so. So us blending would either be a disaster or beautifully horrendous for us and everyone around us. But, by chance, we ended up as... something else. We turned out to be horrible perfection.

Yeah, sure. We had ups and downs, but doesn't everything?

In the end we survived me endangering him, me leaving Neverland twice, a chemist with a bomb, two kidnappings, blackmail, torture, feuds, thievery, rudeness, snoops, hatred, control, murder, amnesia, and just life

We are like fire. We are beautiful, powerful, and regal. But we are also deadly, destructive, and merciless.

Our love is a soft rainfall where small water droplets slide down the glass in a melancholy sort of way: Lovely but also sad

Our love is sitting by the fire alone cuddled in a blanket with hot chocolate: Comforting, but also lonely.

Our love is a quiet night: peaceful, but also depressing

Our love is a memory of someone deceased: Pleasant but also awful

Our love is a vacant room, reading: Magical, but also upsetting

Our love is eating alone: Quiet but also mournful

Our love is a slow song: Enchanting, but also painful

And I know that I love him, and I am certain he loves me, even if we aren't the couple out of romance novels.

We may not have firework kisses all the time.

We may not cuddle on the couch in the winter.

We may not defy our parents to be together.

We may not sneak out at midnight and meet at "the spot"

We may not get married.

We may not have children.

We may not run away together.

But we have true, genuine, real love. And love never bends the way you want it. So you may not look at us and think we actually love each other, but we do. Even if you can't see it.

And no, our love isn't always perfect. But it's real.

We have what some may call horrible perfection.

I love Peter Pan, the voice inside my head.

The End.

CPSIA information can be obtained
at www.ICGtesting.com
Printed in the USA
LVHW080138191222
735289LV00011BA/2520